Never Forsaken
The Journey to See God

Destiney Watson

Weeping Eye Entertainment Productions

Dedicated to the love who changed my life

This kind of love is spiritual
The kind of love that takes courage

Courage to choose someone each and every day not knowing
if they will be as frustrated with you as you are sometimes

This kind of love is spiritual
The kind of love that takes courage

Courage to trust in the God that placed you together

That He would wrap His loving arms around you both in
moments of despair and agony

That He would give you forever and always with this person
that has the same courage as you

This kind of love is spiritual
Binding since the creation of the earth

This kind of love is spiritual, God ordained, Heaven
authorized

The kind of love in which the idea of love shall be
revolutionized

Intro

In my life, seeing God has been a constant battle. Battling trauma and pain that would cause the average woman to fold has caused me to understand what it means to be a survivor. My endurance through molestation, rejection, neglect, and abandonment have led me to this very moment.

> *I, Agatha Cole, know that I am ill-equipped to raise this baby, but in this moment, I know that my God is. In this moment, I forgot that I hated God.*

As I gaze upon the face of the life God has allowed me to birth into this world, I now know that God has never forsaken me. It has all been a part of His plan.

But... as I stand here... terrified, alone and confused. There is another level of dependability required of a mother; I haven't even learned the basic functions of being an adult, nor was I reliable enough to depend on myself.

Regardless of what I don't know about being an adult, being a wife, and now being a mother, there is one thing I know for certain... this tiny human being depends on me. Panic and anxiety strike my heart in the worst way as my eyes analyze my sweet angel. The curvatures of his face, reflective of mine and my husband's. The swirl of our love, reflective in each of his facial features. Feeling warmth travel down my cheek, I sigh. The first tear opened the floodgates for a barrage of tears to sprint down my face.

I pace the floor, my sweet angel swaddled in his nighttime blanket, my arms swaying back and forth, attempting to soothe him. I realize that my attempts to soothe him are more comforting for myself.

I need God.

I hate to need Him. My life has been one tragic struggle after another, and experience has taught me that God only hears when He wants. *That has to be the answer.* But, I cannot deny that in this moment of despair, something is calling me to seek Him again.

The small voice I hear prompting me to pray, echoes through the loud thoughts urging me against it. There is no denying it any longer. The more I look upon my sweet angel's face, the more I long to give him the best of me. In this moment, completely dependent upon God. I have no other choice, but to trust that by praying and believing that He will see us through.

"God, I have no idea what I am supposed to do with this baby. God, help me raise this child. I could not see you in my life, but right now I need to see *You,* Lord," I wailed, in desperation as my mind raced over the events I endured in my youth and my inability to see God in those moments.

Those moments where I looked to heaven and prayed for God to rescue me. Those moments where I did like Mother told me and called on Jesus, but He never answered. Those moments when it was of a greater benefit to me to slip away from my body because it was better to be numb to what was happening than to be conscious of the events taking place. These thoughts were swirling around in my mind and gave way to a roaring wave of despair telling me "this is all pointless" and "God is not listening."

Suddenly, I stopped wailing.

My life has been one tragic struggle after another.

I have prayed and received no guidance.

I have pleaded and received no mercy.

I have petitioned and received nothing but silence.

Maybe God has forsaken me.

Just as I am losing faith, my sweet angel snuggles closer to me. I can tell he is awaking. His little body squirming in my arm provides a momentary relief from my turmoil. He opens his eyes, smiles at me, and it illuminates everything in my world. I nestle my baby closer to my bosom and call on the name of Jesus.

"Jesus!" I exclaim, through a soft sob. "Thank you for answering my prayers. Thank you for allowing me to see you. I see you in my sweet angel!" The tears trickle from my eyes again. As I pray, I feel something shift on the inside of me.

"You granted us this angel! I praise you, Lord for this angel! How so many are unable, you blessed me to deliver a healthy baby! When so many husbands are reluctant to stand up and be present, you have blessed me with a man after your own heart! Thank you, God!" I could feel my body gaining strength as I prayed.

"You are showing me that you have not forsaken me right now, and I believe you have not forsaken me! I believe you are here with me! I believe you, God! I believe that you have laid out the path for us to follow! I believe that path will be exactly as you said in your word, Lord..."

I feel as if my body is crumbling into a million pieces and being rebuilt right where I stand. And in that moment, a burning fire started bubbling up inside of me that I had never felt before.

"God, I know you said that your plan is to prosper us! God, I am sorry that I strayed so far away from your love and tender care! Thank you for reminding me of who you are! Thank you for never giving up on me, even when I gave up on you! Thank you for sticking with me even when I wanted nothing to do with you! Thank you, God for your loving kindness towards me! God, my life could have gone another way! You could have ended my life when I tried. You could have taken me out when I sat in that kitchen floor with that knife in my hand, ready to cut myself out of your story. But I thank you! Glory to your name for saying, "No!" And right now, I say 'yes.' I say 'yes' to whatever you want to do through me! I say 'yes' to what you want me to do! I say 'yes' to who you want me to be — the best wife, mother, sister, friend, and daughter! Where I can't, I believe you can! Thank you for showing yourself mighty in my life!"

I gaze down at my sweet angel and see he has drifted into the most peaceful sleep, even as I am wailing and praying. He remains unbothered by what is going on. It is almost as if he knows that no matter what is going on, he has no reason to fear or lose sleep because I protect him. He doesn't have to worry about what is happening around him because he is safe in the arms of someone who loves him unconditionally.

"Thank you, God," I whisper through my tears, as I kiss the forehead of my sweet angel. I just saw God because of you, sweet angel. And I will make sure that you see Him in everything you do. May God bless you and keep you... in Jesus' name I pray, Amen."

Chapter 1 - Born for Slaughter

Born in a time where the world was not made for people like me — people with skin that radiates golden in the sunlight and radiates a deep hue of brown in the moonlight — I was just as cursed with melanin as I was with femininity. The curvature of my bosom accentuated by the small size of my waist only magnified the shape of my birthing hips. From a very young age, I hated God for the suffering these mere features caused me. I was born in a time where men were not held accountable for their actions, no matter how deplorable. Born in a time where the world does not chastise men for their lustful thoughts of me, but chastises me for my God-given features. I grew up feeling I was forever cursed for being who God created me to be.

I was not a girl. I was not a person. I was merely flesh; flesh that was ripe for the slaughter, and I hated God for the slaughter He left me to endure.

Knowing what I know, I should have expected nothing different from what happened this faithful autumn morning.

It was cool outside, and I could hear the harmonious sounds of the birds chirping near my bedroom window; it being such a pleasant sound. Like any other day, I was just about to start my daily routine with getting my sister and brother up, getting them bathed and dressed so that Mother could sleep in. It was just the four of us.

My Mother was a strong black woman unafraid to speak her mind and incapable of showing true motherly affection. My brother James, in all of his middle child splendor, was a shy boy of few words. He was more concerned with building monsters in his room from the time he finished his homework until dinner, and then once more before bedtime. My youngest sibling, Lucille, was the most vocal of us all. She took after Mother in the way she could sass. Her teachers always mentioned her being a 'social butterfly' when they would ask to speak to Mother.

Mother took care of us all on her own. My father wasn't around and my younger siblings' dad, Paul, was stationed in the military overseas.

Mother worked nights at the Pink Lady Cafeteria — long nights that kept food on our table and clothes on our backs. She was not to be disturbed until she felt like being disturbed. That time would usually come after she downed a pint of whiskey after brushing her teeth and showering. Until then, it was my responsibility to ensure that everyone in the house was ready and presentable for Mother's inspection. I never questioned Mother. I never needed to. She was Mother, and she did as she saw fit; we were sure to never make her fuss.

"Aggie, you want to help me out?" asked my cousin Thomas on this faithful autumn morning.

He made my skin crawl with the way he said my name. It wasn't until much later that I realized just how weird it was, and it was an *unusually* disgusting crawl. He was 16 years old at the time, older than me by five years.

"Thomas, not now," I scolded. "I have to get James and Lucille up and ready before Mother gets up and starts moving."

He stood in the doorway of my room, one hand firmly on the doorpost with the other hand resting on the inseam of his pants, "C'mon Aggie, this will only take as long as you let it."

Pulling my robe tighter around my waist, I made my way towards him, "Thomas, that is gross! You're my cousin. Now, MOVE!" I was mildly strident, but not so much that I heard my voice crack, and I knew I didn't want to wake Mother. She would kill us both.

As I pushed my way through the open door, Thomas attempted to stop me. But he also knew that if we woke Mother up, there would be hell to pay. He quickly retreated to his room. That's one situation I never wanted to explain to Mother. We were living in a time where proper ladies did not have such things happen to them unless they welcomed it.

Once James and Lucille were up and dressed properly, it was also my job to prepare their breakfast and to clean up their area. Afterwards, I walked them to primary school. Their school was only a quarter mile from the middle school, so I dropped them off and picked them up every day.

Each afternoon, we'd walk home together, and they would tell me all about their day and they would ask me about middle school. They are so eager to get to middle school, I would spend most of our conversation trying to convince them otherwise.

When we arrived home, Mother was preparing dinner. "Hey, my babies!" she said, as she greeted James and Lucille. Her deep eyes were piercing right through mine even as her mouth smiled. "Agatha, come 'round the back and help me gather the clothes. Lucille and James, get out your homework and l will check it when I come back in."

"Yes, Mother," they sang in unison.

I jolted when the screen door slammed behind us. "What are you jumping for, Agatha?" she inquired, as she kept walking.

"No reason, I was just startled by the screen door." I stooped to pick up the clothes basket.

"Agatha? What was Thomas doing at your bedroom door this morning? You know it is not proper for a young man to be in a young woman's bedroom that time of morning..."

Mother was taking clothes down from the line as I followed her with the clothes basket. "It was nothing Mother, he was asking me something."

"Mmm, hmm... well, don't let it happen again. It just ain't proper for a young lady to entertain a young man at her bedroom door. Take that to the common area."

"Yes, ma'am. Sorry to disturb you. It won't happen again." I knew it wouldn't be the last time, but there was nothing left to be said. Mother's mind was already made up about the situation.

Chapter 2 - The Emotional Trinity

My 13th birthday came and went in a blur of confusion, rage and sadness. Until this point, it was as if I had erased my prior existence. It was like I had become someone else, or at least that is what my mother made it seem like.

"Agatha!" she shouted, as she whacked my leg with the newspaper. "Agatha! Do you know what time it is?"

I, in fact, knew that it was time for me to get up to get James and Lucille ready for school. But I didn't feel like it. My entire body ached.

What Mother didn't know is that for the past several weeks, since his return from camp, Thomas had become more aggressive in his pursuit of me and even though it had been years since his first attack, my entire essence yearned to cease to exist.

He came home from a high school party one night in a drunken stupor, with the stench of liquor radiating through his pores and filling the air. I awoke to him whispering, "Happy Birthday, Aggie."

His large hand covered my mouth before I could process what was happening. I was in shock, frozen with fear. Thomas knew that with my door shut, no one could hear what was going on, and if Mother found out, she would blame me and believe that it was my fault. He used that knowledge to his advantage.

With one forceful hand over my mouth, he quickly used the other to reach his pants. I closed my eyes tight and waited for it to be over. I figured that fighting would have only made it worse. I kept telling myself that once he was finished, the worse would be over. My bedrail made the most faint creaking sound against the wall, but it helped to lull my anxiety. I imagined it to be the soothing sound of ocean waves hitting the side of rocks by the pier. Can you visualize it? Do you hear it, too? I felt the cool breeze and sea mist rushing over my face, with the warmth of the sun filling my soul and the sand between my toes. It made my heart sing.

I laid there in silence, and for a minute I could hear my mother saying, "Sometimes, I hate that I need God. Life shouldn't be so hard." I get it now! *Where is He? I need Him now and He is nowhere to be found! Life shouldn't be so hard for me to need a God who doesn't come when I want Him. I need Him now!*

My eyes were heavy with tears as they opened. In an instant, it was over, and Thomas was gone, but traces of him lingered in areas that I could never erase.

What a way to start a birthday. I never imagined this to be a burden of turning 13! I had an agonizing ache that I had never felt. A feeling that I would never wish on anyone in life.

Chapter 3 - My Raggedy Mother

It was around mid-October when James and Lucille's dad returned home from the Army. I could not remember a time when Mother was so happy. We were elated to have him back. With Paul around, this allowed Mother to work fewer hours at the Pink Lady, as he was getting his military benefit checks every month. Mother didn't have to work, but she couldn't bear the thought of not having her own money.

Four months had passed since that ragged night with Thomas. But he continued to force himself onto me. It didn't matter whether I was in the basement doing laundry or sorting through things in the garage, he would even pretend to fix things around the house so that he could roam freely without Mother questioning him.

With all of the excitement around Paul's arrival, there was no time to deal with my sorrow of being repeatedly molested. I kept it to myself. *Why should I say something? Who could I open up to?* It would only lead to my family hating me, attacking me with shame, and I already hated myself...enough for them all.

Paul was an amazing father to James and Lucille, and he loved the hell out of Mother, *literally*. She seemed more nurturing than ever before. She was waking up early and cooking breakfast in the mornings. On days that Paul would go to his veteran's meetings, she'd even spend a couple of afternoons taking us to the park after school. When Lucille asked Paul about his meetings, he would tell her they were to make sure that he stayed happy because sometimes being at war can make people sad. He was right — war was ugly and brutal. It left you empty and sad.

I was reluctant to have Paul around, not because he had given me a reason to 'be', but simply because he was a man. My reluctancy remained unnoticed, Mother was head over heels for him as she had always been. His picture was perched on her bedside table. Paul had such a hold on Mother that she even picked up an interest in being more interactive with me. It was to protect her own social image, but we bonded. The fact that he caused Mother to desire a closer bond with her own daughter is a thought I never cared to give energy to. It did not matter to me the surrounding pretenses behavioral shift.

"Agatha, dear, don't you think we should update your wardrobe? You used to love dresses and pretty colors," expressed Mother. "Now, it just seems like you are hiding in those baggy black clothes. And your hair... your hair has always been so luscious! It is a tangled-up mess, dear. You are far too young to let yourself look raggedy."

That was a great way to put it, Mother. I feel raggedy — useless.

We had Paul's credit card, so I let her buy whatever her heart desired. *It didn't mean that I had to wear it.* There was no amount of pretty clothes that could take away these ugly feelings inside of me. *Why did God make me like this?*

Was life as good as Mother was making it look? It seemed to only be getting worse.

Chapter 4 - The Density of Numbness

Life was just passing us by, and Paul had been making Mother the happiest woman alive. He told my siblings and I that he would move us out of our country shack and into a fancy new house in the town center. James and Lucille ate up his every word. I did not trust his words. Words had proven to me to be useless in the past 16 years. Words meant nothing; actions are what I learned to rely on.

A few years into their courtship, Paul married Mother and bought us a new house in the town center. It was a white house with green shutters on the windows and a brown door. Town center was on the rise and had buzzing businesses all up and down Main Street. Day in and day out, you could find people strutting their Sunday best trying to be seen. The atmosphere in the town center moved at a faster pace than in the country. Everything and everyone was fast. The cars, the conversation, even the money.

I never asked how he could afford our new house because I am sure if I dared to question it, Mother would not be pleased. But Paul came into money more quickly than any person I had ever met before.

Mother even quit the Pink Lady to pursue her passion as a seamstress. Paul said she didn't have to work another day in her life, but Mother rebutted with, "As long as I love what I do, it won't be work and it will keep us off the streets."

She created beautiful, air-gasping pieces and business seemed to be fantastic for her, especially since Paul's army buddies were her biggest clients; they were always buying fancy things for their wives and girlfriends.

Thomas, you wonder? Yea… was no longer living with us. Unfortunately, not because of what he'd done to me, but because he had enlisted in the army. They had caught him drinking at an event and when confronted, he spazzed out and stabbed a security guard who was trying to send him home. The lawyer Paul hired recommended that Thomas go to the Army to sort through his aggression. This was a moment to live for — I could breathe.

For James and Lucille, they were elated having their mother and father together again. It was a welcoming change — James' grades improved, plus he'd started behaving better in school and he was building fewer monsters in his room. I loved that Lucille is blossoming; she's started being more kind in her social interactions. There was less sass in her demeanor. She even mentioned becoming a journalist with her new (and only) friend Michelle in New York one day. *Oh, the joy to see my babies growing up right before my eyes!*

For me, it'd been six long years since my last traumatic experience. Six long years to push through my pain. Six long years to forget about Thomas and his heavy, rugged body on mine. Six long yea — *suddenly, the phone rang.* I overheard Mother on the phone planning to pick someone up, but anxiously, I wondered who...

Could it be...? How... could it be? I wasn't sure.

Once she arrived back at the house, I heard the car door slam. The front door creaked loudly as it opened. "Aggie, James, Lucy... come on down and say hey to your cousin."

Thomas was back. For a moment, I felt a shortness of breath in my lungs. How could God forsake me by letting him come back? *How!*

I had worked so hard to bury his existence. Even when Mother took his phone calls, I tried to make myself scarce during those times. There was absolutely nothing that I needed to say to him. What could I possibly say? Sometimes it worked, but there would be times where Mother insisted that I talk. She'd say, "Family needs each other to make it through the tough times."

What a load of bullshit! We weren't family! He was a molester, and I was a victim! I wanted nothing to do with him! I was angry!

There I stood, 16-years-old and devastated. I just knew I had surpassed this phase of my life. There he stood, right in front of me — a 21-year-old man. I had hoped he would be in there for life! I had hoped he would rot behind enemy lines and I would never have to see him again.

But here he was, right in front of me.

"Hey Aggie," he spoke in a booming voice. There were a million thoughts racing through my mind. I felt like everyone's eyes were on me, wondering why I was so frigid towards this 'stranger'. To make matters worse, it was Thanksgiving! It's supposed to be a joyful day.

He was family, right? Holidays made the family come together, right? Good Christian attribute number three is a loving family, right?

The rustling of the leaves outside and the cool air always made the holiday seem a little more comfy. It's the comfort that has always made fall my favorite season. The laughter of family, the smell of spices and the warmth that comes from family gatherings is soothing to the mind, for most *normal* people. But what is normal? I don't feel normal. My mind was everywhere, and I could not silence the voices in my head. The anxiety swirled so high that I made myself sick. I thought, *"God, this can't be actual life All the joy, smiles and laughter... how is this happening while I'm dying on the inside? Do you not see me! Do you not care? God, why have You forsaken me!"*

And then suddenly, I wasn't sick. It was as if the veil over my mind had been lifted. I was no longer sick, nor anxious.

At that moment, I felt a surge of numbness come over me. I created a mental tarp to drape over my anxieties about certain situations. This mental covering allowed me to carry on as if life was normal. I didn't need to process emotions.

I became a walking zombie. A facade. A skeleton devoid of most human emotions. I could function where necessary in the capacity that pleased whoever I was aiming to please. I was good at helping people accomplish something. That became the focus of my mind.

As long as I was focusing on helping the surrounding people, I would not have to deal with what was underneath the tarp.

The tarp made it so easy to forget that I was a victim of trauma. It allowed me to recreate myself separate from my experiences. With Thomas gone and the tarp covering his body, I didn't need human emotions. I only needed to keep helping people.

Helping people allowed me to skate through emotions when other catastrophic events happened in my life. I was so busy doing things to help people, that I didn't have time to wallow in my emotions. I would feel enough to make people comfortable, and then I would be back to the grind of taking on everyone else's burdens.

I never had to tap into my emotions and feelings. The tarp plus keeping busy made for a numbness too dense to process certain emotions. Emotions that I did not care to process were suppressed and forgotten.

I was numb.

When Thomas returned back into duty after the holidays, I later received word that he'd been tragically injured while fighting overseas, I felt nothing.

Remorse...joy...sadness...anger...none of it.

I threw him and all of our encounters under the tarp and kept on with my life.

The tarp allowed me to forget about his heinous crimes against my body and keeping busy kept my actual focus on the tasks at hand.

It's no wonder how my life donned this rotation of unwarranted abuse.

I just kept throwing the incidents under the tarp as if they never happened. I never allowed my brain to cope with any of the trauma. I felt this made me powerful. I could be unaffected by things that happened to me, but little did I know I was dooming myself to this continuous cycle of confusion, rage and sadness. The same trio of emotions I felt that faithful autumn morning, and every incident that has occurred since then.

Chapter 5 - Poison is the Remedy

Thomas isn't my only painful memory. Between 14 and 16-years-old, there was Cynthia Gaston, my best friend. We were inseparable.

Cynthia made me feel things that I didn't know were possible. She made me feel dirty, yet desirable simultaneously. The tarp over my mind allowed me to dive deeper into believing that if I *'just let it happen, it would soon stop.'* Whew, these tarps... they were like Novocaine to my brain. I was numb to all desires of my own and only lived to fulfill the desires of whoever showed an interest in me.

I had become numb to my own needs for safety and comfort. That is what Cynthia did for me — made herself a safety net.

When she touched me, I didn't flinch from the pain. I didn't even put up a fight. What was the use in fighting, anyway?

Everyone got what they wanted from me — *except me.*

Our move to the town center distanced me from Cynthia, thus reviving the numbness to my own needs for safety and comfort.

Soon after, there was Imani. She was the person who taught me to be comfortable in being who I am, even when I wasn't myself. She would touch me and would flinch even less than with Cynthia. *Yes, I was uncomfortable, but I didn't care.* She was my friend, and she liked me. That was all I needed — a friend. We shared secrets and giggled, as teenage girls do. It was almost freeing to be in a friendship that I felt benefited me. Here, the benefit outweighed the discomfort.

Our friendship ended when she was shipped off to live with her grandparents because her mother was on drugs. Throughout the duration of our friendship, the mental tarp kept me believing that if I *'just let it happen, eventually it will stop'*. After a while, I just accepted the fact that my life would forever be uncomfortable. One tragic misuse after another was all my life would surmount too, and if it meant I wouldn't be rejected, then I was okay with it.

The tarp portrayed this benefit as greater than the loneliness, pain and shame that I actually felt. The mental covering blurred the lines between being useful and being used. They were my remedy and my poison, keeping me sane and bound.

Throughout my youth there was Thomas, Cynthia, Imani, David, Tremaine, Michael, Richard, and Terrell.

As I maneuvered through life, those names didn't belong to people. *They couldn't!* Because those people would not harm me after professing their love and concern for me. Surely those people would not use me for their own pleasure with no regard for my needs of safety and comfort. Surely, I would not stand by and allow myself to be used. But I did time and time again I was not a girl. I was not a person. I was merely flesh; flesh that was ripe for the slaughter, and I hated God for the slaughter He left me to endure — just paralytic cycling through the motions.

It was under the tarp, so it didn't exist. I would not talk about it, they would not talk about it, so what would be the point in talking about it? This made it easier for it to disappear under the tarp. Not realizing that it had paralyzed me into reliving the same brokenness time and time again.

I knew that coming forward about any of what happened would only lead to questions and emotions that I was ill-equipped to deal with. I had suppressed everything, and the tarp plus busyness kept them covered.

The tarp, the busyness, my silence all a remedy, yet a poison. I kept telling myself, *"If you just let it happen, eventually it will stop... who would believe a reject like you anyway... it will all be over soon."*

Chapter 6 - The Rest is Still Unwritten

As life went on, and as I grew older, I never once thought that I could experience happiness or feelings of healthy desires. His name was Elliott. When we met, I had no idea how much damage these tarps had done to my psyche.

There was a gaping hole in my faith. I was angry, but I possessed so many good Christian attributes. Some may say it's no excuse, but I still allowed the enemy to consume my mind with my ties to the past trauma. It manifested itself in ways that I could not explain before meeting Elliott. I was a perpetual victim of my past. Going through the motions and telling myself to just let it happen.

I had been living life thinking that I was free from my past. The tarps kept the traumatic incidents hidden from view. So I could believe that although those things happened to me, I was no longer affected by them. All the while, the enemy had taken my trauma and repackaged it as a lack of boundaries. I allowed people to say what they wanted and called it "being nice". I gave up so much more just to compensate for other people's lack and called it benevolence.

These things were my past traumas, and I truly needed healing.

My love for Elliott made me want to give him the best of me, so I did the work to ensure I was where God needed me to be in order to give him the love that he deserved. My relationship with Elliot prompted me to dig deeper within myself to allow that inner healing.

I wanted him to get to know the real Agatha. Not the skeleton facade I had been parading around as for most of my youth.

I needed to allow Elliott to do what it is he wanted to do... love me.

Elliott wanted to love away my pain. He wanted to love me exactly for who I was, with all of my flaws. It was such a foreign concept to me. I had spent my entire life hiding from my own flaws and keeping them a secret from anyone who tried to love me.

Elliott's love for me, made me want to destroy the tarp and all of the grief and trauma that lied underneath it.

I saw God's love for me within Elliott.

It was in the challenges that God was equipping me. I learned that the tarps were a tactic of the enemy to keep me bound in my trauma. To me I thought the tarp was protecting me from pain, but all the while, God was trying to draw purpose from my pain.

Though our love has not been perfect, it has been everything I needed to find out who I am and to realize that God has never forsaken me.

Giving God my pain allowed Him to make it purposeful instead of painful. God knew that I would endure before it would equip me to be who He called me to be.

In my foolish attempt at running my own life, I made it harder than it needed to be. I allowed the enemy to trick me into believing that by hiding my secrets, I had power over them. In reality, it was the exact opposite. True healing does not come from hiding, but from exposing the pain for what it is...

A necessary step in God's plan.

God has a purpose for everything. Our responsibility as faithful believers is to seek peace in our purpose — even in our pain.

Pain without God will always remain painful, even when you try to cover it up. *Pain with God will be purposeful*, and He will use it to be a light for someone else.

I wish life as a Christian was simple and that we wouldn't have to endure any pain, but when we look for God in our pain, we realize it is never for our benefit, but for His glory.

This story is still being written, and I already know it will have its share of trauma, but I will seek to see my Source in it all because *'life shole ain't easy'*.

Thank you, God that I am *'Never Forsaken.'*

About the author

Born in a small town in rural North Carolina, Destiney knew from an early age she was 'different'. Always feeling inadequate among her friends because she didn't want to do the things they did, go the places they went, or be around the people they were around, Destiney's love for words became her escape from reality.

A teacher by profession, Destiney is also a motivational speaker, business owner/found, event coordinator, and anything else God leads her to do. Destiney refuses to ascribe to a particular niche, and prides herself in being a "one woman under God" show.

Destiney's mission to empower women carries over into her non-profit, Bougie Busy Inc. and her business, Destined for Greatness Consulting, where she trains and motivates women of faith to dismantle bloodline traumas and generate dynasty wealth.

Readers connect with Destiney through the candid tone in which she writes. Regardless of the genre, Destiney doesn't hold back. You can count on page turning stories in every book she produces.